The Crackin' Crimbo Book

Bubblegum

An essential *Bubblegum* guide

Ged Backland and Phil Renshaw

■SCHOLASTIC

THUMPA THUMPA THUMPA THUMPA THUMPA THUMPA

With thanx to Jez Spencer, Ben Whittington, Keith Auty and all at Carlton Cards

Scholastic Children's Books
Commonwealth House, 1-19 New Oxford Street
London WC1A 1NU
a division of Scholastic Ltd
London ~ New York ~ Toronto ~ Sydney ~ Auckland
Mexico City ~ New Delhi ~ Hong Kong

First published in the UK by Scholastic Ltd, 2001
Copyright © Carlton Cards Ltd, 2001
ISBN 0 439 99475 6

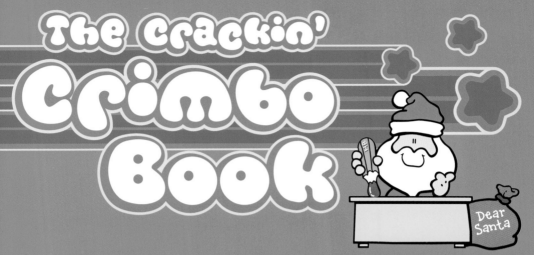

The Crackin' Crimbo Book

All you need to know about Crimbo ...

Welcome to the Bubblegum Crackin' Crimbo Book. If you want to find out what festive frolics Xmas Diva, Crimbo Pud or Festive Floozy get up to, then this is the one book you'll need to get your mitts on. Chill out with Frostee, find out where Party Animal is most likely to be and discover Rosco's favourite colour. Fancy cooking up some groovy Crimbo snacks for your bezzy mates? Then check out the Crimbo Crew's rockin' recipes. Find out if YOU could be a Groovy Santa, or just relax with the cool pages packed choc-full of puzzles. All in all, it's everything you need to have the bestest ever Yule. So sit back, chill out and turn a few pages in the company of the coolest Crimbo Crew around!

Groovy Santa

Groovy Santa is just that
a real cool groovy guy
You'll find him late on Crimbo Eve
groovin' thru' the sky

Groovy Santa is cooler than the North Pole where he lives. He gets all the reindeer grooving thru' the snow by putting on his ghetto blaster and belting out a cool Crimbo tune. You'll find him dancin' and groovin' anywhere he can.

Most likely to be...

Groovin' on your roof

Most likely to say...

Have a groovy Crimbo!

Fave Colour

Snow White (of course!)

Groovy Santa is real ace
Watch him groove all over the place!

Crimbo Totty

She's a glam chick all cool 'n' fine
she drives all the guys potty
It's clear to see they all want to be
with the gal called Crimbo Totty!

Crimbo Totty is hot stuff. She's glammed up to the nines and looks a million dollars in her spesh Crimbo frock. She's always got a queue of people waiting for a kiss. This gal is goooooooorgeous!

Most likely to be...

Under the mistletoe

Most likely to say...

No thanks

Fave Colour

Blushing Pink

Crimbo Totty you can't miss
'Cos there's a line of boys all wantin' a kiss

Crimbo Pud

He sits in front of the box
at being lazy he's real good
With a full belly in front of the telly
he's a proper Crimbo Pud!

Crimbo Pud is a lazy article. He'd sit in front of the telly all Crimbo if the gang would let him. He's content watching the footy and stuffing his face with turkey sarnies. All in all he's a proper Crimbo couch potato!

Most likely to be...

On the couch watching the goggle box

Most likely to say...

Make us a cuppa

Fave Colour

Black and White

Crimbo Pud loves to see
You bringing him a cup of tea

Xmas Diva

When she hits the dance floor
she gets that Crimbo fever
She's delightful and delicious
she's a groovin' Xmas Diva

Xmas Diva is what Crimbo is all about. Letting her hair down and grabbing the limelight as she hits the floor on a mission to groove to some smashin' toons. She's the life of the party, the soul of the dance floor. She's the absolute queen of sparkle!

Most likely to be... ✳

Dancin' her pins off

Most likely to say... ✳

Hey Mr DJ put a record on

Fave Colour ✳

Crimbo Red

THUMPA
THUMPA
THUMPA
THUMPA
THUMPA
THUMPA

When Xmas Diva hits the floor
The DJ pumps the toons up more!

Crimbo Nutter

Waaaaaaaaaaaaaaaaaaaa

I'm mad me I am!

Crimbo Nutter is just that
totally gone it's said
Rumour is when she was young
she got dropped on her head

There's never a dull moment when Crimbo Nutter is about. Always one for practical jokes, you'd better watch out she doesn't fill your wellies with custard or put sprouts in your coat pockets. Despite her nuttiness everyone loves her, so she gets to go to all the parties.

Most likely to be...

Running round in your nan's wig

Most likely to say...

Waaaaaaaaaa!

Fave Colour

White with green squiggles
(well she is mad!)

BOOM!

I'm mad me I am!

Crimbo Nutter is just ace
She runs around all over the place

Top Chick

She's just so flippin' lovely
she makes all the boys love-sick
She's spesh and ace with an angel's face
she's a totally gorge Top Chick

Top Chick is a really nice gal. She's everyone's best friend and will keep all
your secrets safe and will listen to all your problems. She's totally gorgeous
too and has lots of boys wanting to hold her hand. Lucky gal!

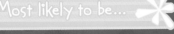

Most likely to be...

Listening to a friend

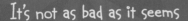

Most likely to say...

It's not as bad as it seems

Fave colour

Warm Pink

Top Chick is such a gal
You feel so lucky if she's your pal

Crimbo Dude

Crimbo Dude is very cool
in his bestest Crimbo clothes
He'll chat so calm upon his phone
with his specs upon his nose

Crimbo Dude is cooler than the turkey on Boxing Day morning. He always gets his Crimbo clothes right and looks the part wherever he goes. He's so laid back nothing ever ruffles his super-cool persona, except of course a peck on the cheek from Top Chick under the mistletoe.

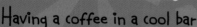

Most likely to be...

Having a coffee in a cool bar

Most likely to say...

Happy Day Dude

Fave Colour

Cool Blue

Crimbo Dude is cool and hip
Cooler than the iceberg that hit that ship!

Festive Floozy

She makes the boys go ga ga
one kiss sends them all woozy
She's really ace with a snogable face
she's a dahling Festive Floozy

Festive Floozy is the Dahling of the Crimbo Bubblegum crew. She's always got a sprig of mistletoe handy and will never miss an opportunity to snog a lush lad. She's a bit dotty and forgetful, so some lucky boys end up getting two kisses in one day (Lucky Fellas).

Most likely to be...

Under the mistletoe

Most likely to say...

Kiss me quick

Fave Colour

Kissing Pink

Watch out boyz for Festive Floozy
One quick kiss will send you woozy

Party Animal

Party Animal loves a do
it's plain he loves to dance
Trouble is once he starts
he ends up in his pants

Party Animal really loves to party. He's partying when most of us are tucked up in bed for the night. Never one to miss an opportunity for a knees-up he spends all Crimbo dancing and making merry.

Most likely to be...

At the best party

Most likely to say...

Coming to the do?

Fave Colour

Party Purple

Party Animal never stops
From party to party he flippin' pops!

Wild Child

When it comes to Crimbo
she's never meek or mild
She's flippin' nuts, no if's or but's
a proper mad Wild Child

Crimbo was made for Wild Child. She loves all the parties and the mad singing. She especially likes dancing with her mad rellies. She's always first up in the morning and last to bed at night. Don't be surprised if you find her groovin' with Santa on Crimbo Eve.

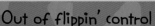

Most likely to be...

Out of flippin' control

Most likely to say...

Let's party!

Fave Colour

Lime Green

Wherever there's a Crimbo do
That's where you'll find Wild Child too

Frostee Snowman

Frostee's just the coolest
he's well chilled and he's ace
With eyes of coal and a carrot nose
and a great big smiley face

Frostee is, quite literally, the coolest member of the Bubblegum Xmas crew.
He spends most of Crimbo outdoors 'cos he doesn't like getting too hot, but
he never gets lonely — the rest of the gang won't let him. Besides, he's always
got lots to do, including throwing the odd snowball at Old Git!

Most likely to be...

Chilling out

Most likely to say...

Here comes a snowball!

Fave Colour

Ice Blue

Hang with him and you'll see why
Frostee is the coolest guy!

Rosco Robin

Rosco Robin's really sweet
a happy cheerful chap
He stays real cool all thru' Yule
and never gets in a 'flap'!

Rosco is the smallest member of the crew — but also one of the loudest.
He loves to belt out Crimbo tunes at the top of his voice — unfortunately
for the gang, it's usually at 4 o'clock in the morning! Because he's so cute
though, no one really minds and they all luv him to bits.

Most likely to be...

Chillin' in a tree

Most likely to say...

I'm dreaming of a white Christmas (loudly!)

Fave Colour

Redbreast Red (of course!)

Rosco loves a Crimbo song
He'll sing all bloomin' Crimbo long!

Boy Racer

Diamond Geezer

Old Git

Nutty Tart

Dancing Queen

Happenin' Babe

Stuck? Check out the answers at the back of the book

What * am * I?

Solve these clues to find out the answer,
taking one letter from each clue...

My first is in TREE but not in PINE

My second's in WINTER and also in WINE

My third is in MISTLETOE and KISSING too

My fourth is in SNOWY but not in IGLOO

My fifth is in CRIMBO PUD and in COOL DUDE

My sixth is in FROSTEE but not found in FOOD

My seventh's in SLAP HEAD and DANCING QUEEN too

My eighth is in REDBREAST but not in ICE BLUE

When added together the words that you spy
at Crimbo time maybe you'll see in the sky

Stuck? Check out the answers at the back of the book

Write the answers to the clues in the boxes to reveal what everyone luvs getting at Crimbo...

1.
2.
3.
4.
5.
6.
7.
8.

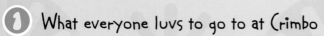

1. What everyone luvs to go to at Crimbo
2. The 'coolest' member of the crew
3. Got no hair but doesn't care
4. What Crimbo Pud is
5. Bit of a 'Diamond'
6. Been known to enjoy himself
7. Where Groovy Santa lives
8. The loudest member of the gang

Stuck? Check out the answers
at the back of the book

crackin' crimbo search

Can you find all the cool Crimbo words listed in the grid opposite? The unused letters will spell out a hidden Crimbo message!

North Pole
Bell
Cracker
Snowballs
Yule
Cool
Party Animal
Ice
Balloon
Prezzie
Chillin'
Rosco
Snowy
Turkey
Wild Child
Top Chick
Mistletoe
Groovy Santa
Crimbo Pud
Crimbo
Xmas Diva
Frostee
Joy

H S L D U P O B M I R C A G
V N E O K C I H C P O T X R
T O H E O S Y W O N S M M O
N W C R A C K E R A C S A O
I B H I B E L L N O D S V
L A G E C Y E K R U T L D Y
L L S I E T C N R I Y I I S
I M B O E E V O E R H V A
H S F J O Y T R O O M C A N
C R I M B O T S H E L D B T
U M I S T L E T O E B L B A
E L O P H T R O N R L I A E
G U E I Z Z E R P M F W C B
R P A R T Y A N I M A L E W

Stuck? Check out the answers at the back of the book

A Recipe For A Groovy Crimbo

Cooking can be tricky
of course we understand
So if you are uncertain
let some grown-ups lend a hand

Frostee's Smashin' Snowman Snacks

Ingredients

8 cups of Popcorn
6 cups of Marshmallows
6 tbsps Butter
Sweets for decoration

Here's Frostee's real spesh recipe
for snowman snacks to eat
They're mega yummy and totally scrummy
a tip-top Crimbo treat

Method

Grease a bowl with some of the butter
Add the popcorn
Melt the marshmallows and butter in a pan
over a medium heat
Stir constantly 'til smooth
Pour over the popcorn
When cool - with buttered-up hands - mould into snowman shapes
Decorate with sweets and put in the fridge to cool and set

And Abracadabra! Your very own snowman snack to serve to your bezzy
mates and nutty rellies. Scrummy!

Rosco's Red-Hot Raspberry Delight

When Winter's bloomin' freezin'
Rosco knows just what to do
He makes this scrummy Crimbo drink
and serves it to the crew

Ingredients

4 cups of milk
8oz white chocolate
1tsp vanilla extract
Raspberries or raspberry syrup
Whipped cream
Grated milk chocolate

Method

Put milk in pan
Heat 'til very hot but not boiling
Remove from heat
Stir in vanilla extract
Add white chocolate in small batches stirring after each
addition until smooth
Ladle into cups and top with raspberries or syrup,
whipped cream and grated chocolate

Hey presto! A scrumb-diddly-umptious Crimbo treat to impress your mates
or that spesh person in your life.

Frostee's Festive Funnies

BOOM!

What have a decorated Xmas tube and Crimbo Nutter got in common?
They're both crackers!

Why can Snowmen see in the dark?
'Cos they've got very good ice-sight!

What is the wettest Crimbo animal?
The Rain-deer

What happened when Crimbo Pud ate some Xmas decorations?
He got tinsel-itis!

Knock! Knock!
Who's there?
Mary
Mary who?
Mary Christmas!

What do the Bubblegum crew sing to Frostee at Crimbo?
'Freeze a jolly good fellow'!

Why does Groovy Santa go down the chimney?
'Cos it 'soots' him!

Knock! Knock!
Who's there?
Wenceslas
Wenceslas who?
Wenceslas bus home!

Crimbo Nutter got a sleeping bag for Xmas...
...then spent two days trying to wake it up!

What's red and brown and goes up and down,
up and down, up and down?
Rosco stuck in a lift!

Can I share your sledge?

Yeah, we'll go halves
You have it uphill and
I'll have it down

CRIMBO RAP

FEAT. MC SNOWY BOOTS & MISSY FROST

Have you ever wanted to write your own cool Crimbo verses?
Well, now you can and it's totally easy peasy! Just pick one line from
each of the boxes in order to create your own funky festive poem.
By choosing different lines, you can soon crank out dozens of poems
to recite to your mates to show them how clever you are!

1

Hope your Crimbo's bonkers

Have the bestest Crimbo ever

Isn't Crimbo flippin' cool

Have a ton of festive frolics

2

With lots of pressies too

And all thru' New Year too

Yes Crimbo's the bestest it's true

Hope Santa's good to you

Have a day that's great wa-hey
So have the maddest ever Yule
It's really clear it's the top time of the year
Have a time that's great with your mates

With pop and goodies too
That's nutty thru' 'n' thru'
You deserve it you flippin' well do!
Chill all Crimbo thru'

Word up!

ALL WRAPPED UP!

Yo!

We've wrapped up the Bubblegum crew!
Read the clues to find who's who...

1
Loopy, mad, no if's or but's
totally bonkers, daft and nuts

2
Who's this person? Do you know?
He's most at home out in the snow

3
All wrapped up in time for Yule
here's a guy who's cooler than cool

4
Always jolly must be said
likes to wear a lot of red

5
This mystery gal loves the limelight
she likes to dance and groove all night

6

Guess where this guy wants to be? Stuffin' his face and watchin' TV

7

The gal the guys all want to meet even wrapped up she looks a treat

8

This mad guy just loves to dance swing his arms and shake his pants

9

A flippin' lovely gorgeous gal guys and girls want to be her pal

10

He's not a turkey, but have you heard our friend's another Crimbo bird!

check out the answers at the back of the book

Get ya pens out!

Groovy Santa's fab 'n' funky flying Cadillac has got stuck in a snowdrift and he's none too chuffed about it. Cheer him up by colouring in these pages while he waits for Rosco Robin to fetch the Bub rescue truck.

Help! We're stuck Santa

ARE YOU A GROOVY SANTA?

1 How often do you change your clothes?

a. Once every forty-three seconds, except on Tuesday and Thursday mornings
   and only then if the Weetabix in your bowl faces North by Northwest.

b. Every day and every night – dancing to all those top tunes gets your
   bell-bottoms right mucky.

c. Never, or once a year. The red suit that you wear is very durable,
   even when you're out grooving all of the time.

2 What colour is your hair?

a. Blue one day, bright green the next.

b. Purple at the moment, but it changes as
   often as the records the DJ spins down at Club Bub.

c. White – after all, you are three hundred and twenty-three years of age.

3 What do you do on Crimbo Eve?

a. Stand on the rooftops in your pants singing carols to the stars.

b. Dance all night down at Club Bub.

c. Deliver presents to three billion people worldwide.

4 Is it cold where you live?

a. Nope – because you eat so many bananas and rush about all the time
   shouting 'cheese biscuits for Prime Minister'.

b. No – too much dancin' going on for you to ever get cold.

c. Freezing! Sometimes even the penguins have to put on woolly pullies.

5 What have you got on your face?

a. A big grin and the remains of a peanut butter and Jelly Baby sandwich.

b. A big smile (because you love everything and everybody).

c. A big white beard.

6 What are your favourite three words?

a. Fish, pig, grommet.

b. Dance, dance, dance.

c. Ho! Ho! Ho!

7 Do you know anyone with a red nose?

a. Loads of people – especially after you've
   pulled it and made a honking sound.

b. Oh dear, no!

c. Yes, a reindeer called Rudolph.

8 What's your fave food?

a. Peanut and Jelly Baby butties.

b. Crisps – salt and vinegar are absolutely the tops!

c. Mince pies washed down with a glass of milk. Mmwwwaaa!

9 How do you travel?

a. By hedgehog!

b. You get Boy Racer to give you a lift in his flash motor, and if he's not
   about Happenin' Babe will always let you jump aboard her Love Bug.

c. By sleigh through the night pulled by reindeer.

10 Have you ever gone into someone's house down the chimney?

a. Yes, all the time – especially when blowing a trumpet.

b. No! Good heavens! It'd mess up your disco clothes.

c. Is there any other way in?

So how did you score?

Mostly (A)

A Groovy Santa you are not. Travelling by hedgehog and eating peanut butter and Jelly Baby sandwiches means you can only be one character ... Crimbo Nutter!

Mostly (B)

If there's anyone less likely to be a Groovy Santa it's you. Although you can groove like him, the red suit is definitely not your cup of tea.

Mostly (C)

Of course you are. But you knew that all along didn't you?

✳ Spot the ✳ Difference

The piccies below aren't as identical as they look.
There are five differences ... can you spot 'em?

Stuck? Check out the answers at the back of the book

Crazy Crimbo Carols
courtesy of
Rockin' Rosco Robin

If you find Crimbo carols naff
then try these out
they'll make you laugh!

To the tune of 'Frosty the Snowman'

Frostee the Snowman
loves the weather when it snows
With his two coal eyes and his woolly hat
and a carrot for his nose.
All the crew luv Frostee
yes he's a flippin' hit
He's totally cool and he luvs Yule
and throws snowballs at Old Git!

To the tune of 'Jingle Bells'

Jingle bells, jingle bells, jingle all the way
oh what fun it is to all chill out on Christmas Day
It's really great, get your mates,
grab your favourite song
Turn the tunes up to full blast
and boogie all night long.

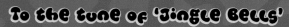

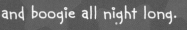

To the tune of 'Silent Night'

Silent night, not tonight
'cos Rosco's singing with all his might
Hear him sing in the early morn',
wakes the crew at the crack of dawn
Rosco Robin sings, Rosco Robin sings.

Silent night, oh what a sight
time for a big snowball fight
Into the fields the crew all go
and at Rosco big snowballs they throw
He'll think twice before singing,
think before he sings.

To the tune of 'We Three Kings'

We're all friends, in the Bubblegum Crew
Cool Dude, Slap Head and Old Git too
Crimbo Pud who's really good
with Frostee and Rosco too.
Oh Diamond Geezer's really cool
there's Nutty Tart the Crimbo fool
They're all here to bring good cheer
and wish you the bestest ever Yule!

WHY NOT JOIN THE FAN CLUB?

If you want to know
more about the crew
then the Fan Club and website's
the place for you!

FANCY BECOMING A MEMBER
OF THE COOLEST CLUB IN TOWN?
WELL IN CASE YOU DIDN'T KNOW,
BUBBLEGUM HAS ITS VERY OWN
FAN CLUB AND WEBSITE.

Come Hang With The Gang

By joining the Bubblegum Fan Club you not only get an exclusive starter pack and 4 issues of your very own magazine a year, but also tons of groovy goodness like:

The Gallery - where YOU can send in your ideas for characters and poems.

Letters page - where you can tell us about yourself, or your nutty mates, or your mad dad, or just chat about anything Bubblegum related.

A penpals section - where you can write to other Bubblegum-mad bods and maybe find yourself a new bezzy mate.

Lots of competitions - where you can get your hands on all the latest Bubblegum goodies plus lots, lots more besides!

Surf's Up!

Have you visited the Bubblegum website yet? If not, why don't you log on at www.bubblegumclub.com for all the latest news, piccies, free games and competitions.

If you fancy getting a dedication on your birthday or maybe setting up a link to your own Bubblegum website, then pay us a visit. Why not send in your own works of art, pay a visit to the Bubblegum arcade and play all the groovy games, or download the latest screensavers and desktop patterns to make your computer bubblicious?

It's all here just waiting for you to log on and get surfing – so don't delay, visit today!

yep! It's...
The Answer Pages

Crazy Crimbo Party

Slap Head   Cool Dude   100% Bad   Diamond Geezer   Boy Racer   Old Git

Nutty Tart   Hunny Bunny   Groovy Chick   Happenin' Babe   Dancing Queen   Disco Diva

What am I?

A reindeer

Crimbo Puzzle

1. Party
2. Frostee
3. Slap Head
4. Lazy
5. Geezer
6. Old Git
7. North Pole
8. Rosco

What everyone luvs getting at Crimbo...

Prezzies

word search

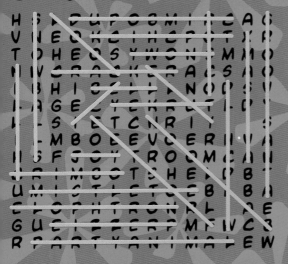

Secret message:
'Have the smashingest Crimbo ever from the Bubblegum Crew'

all wrapped up

1. Crimbo Nutter
2. Frostee
3. Crimbo Dude
4. Groovy Santa
5. Xmas Diva
6. Crimbo Pud
7. Crimbo Totty
8. Party Animal
9. Top Chick
10. Rosco Robin

spot the difference

1. Frostee's flake is missing
2. Stripes not spots on Happenin' Babe's dress
3. Motif on Boy Racer's baseball cap has changed
4. One tree is missing
5. Reindeer has wandered off

who d'ya know in the Crimbo Crew?

Crimbo Pud

Frostee Snowman

Party Animal

Crimbo Dude

Wild Child

Rosco Robin

Xmas Diva

Festive Floozy

Top Chick

Groovy Santa

Crimbo Totty

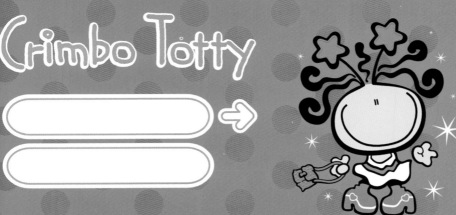

Crimbo Nutter

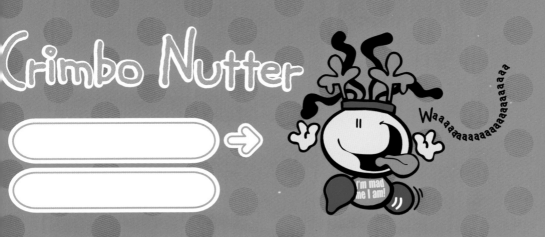

Waaaaaaaaaaaaaaaaaaaaa

I'm mad me I am!

see ya!

A big goodbye, we hope you thought
our Crimbo guide was cool
So now go out and have yourself
the biggest bestest Yule!